FIRST CHAPTER BOOKS

TIME
CHRONICLES

READ WITH
**Biff,
Chip&
Kipper**

A Jack and Three Queens

Written by David Hunt
and illustrated by Alex Brychta

OXFORD
UNIVERSITY PRESS

Before reading

- Read the back cover text and page 5. Which historical person might the Virans be after this time and why?
- Look at page 5. Why do you think art, poetry and plays were very popular in Elizabethan England?

After reading

- Why do you think boy actors played women's characters in Tudor times?

Book quiz

1 Why was this play special?

   a It was the first showing.

   b It was at the Globe theatre.

   c It was being performed for Queen Elizabeth I.

2 Who were the three queens?

3 How did the Virans kidnap the Queen?

See p45 for the book quiz answers!

Before you begin ...

Biff, Chip, Kipper and friends are training to be Time Runners. They are based in the Time Vault, which exists outside time. Their mission is to travel back in time to defeat the Virans, who are trying to destroy history and bring chaos to the future.

The Time Runners have a Zaptrap – a device to capture the Virans – and a Link, which lets them communicate with the Time Vault. Apart from that, they are on their own!

The Globe Theatre
London, 1601

Elizabethan England is sometimes called the Golden Age as
it was a time when art, poetry and plays were very popular.
Almost everyone went to the theatre to see the latest plays.
Perhaps even Queen Elizabeth herself!

Chapter 1

Kipper sat alone in the Games room. He was studying his Time Runner manual. "I'll never remember all this," he muttered.

Suddenly the Time Vault alarm went off.

In Control, Tyler sighed. "What took you so long, Kipper?" he said.

"Sorry," panted Kipper, "I was at the other side of the Vault. What have we got?"

Kipper stared up at the TimeWeb. Tyler pointed to a small spot that looked like a tiny black hole in the fine threads of the web. A faint image appeared in the globe.

"1601," said Tyler. "Somewhere in London."

Kipper strained his memory. "1601? That's um, Queen Elizabeth I, right?"

"Good! So you haven't always been asleep during training then," grinned Tyler.

"Yeah, yeah, Tyler, we can't all be a brainbox like you." Kipper looked around. "Where are the others, anyway?"

"Biff and Wilf have gone already," said Tyler. "Get going."

Chapter 2

Kipper stepped from the portal. Instantly it snapped shut behind him. He felt dizzy, and everything looked blurred. He took off his glasses and rubbed his eyes. Where was he?

After a moment, his eyes focused. Right in front of him was a mighty river busy with boats. It was the River Thames. To his left was a large bridge lined with buildings. "Houses on a bridge?" he thought. "Weird!"

His eyes sharpened. Rising above the low, cramped houses on the opposite bank was a large round building, topped with flags.

A putrid smell filled his nostrils. It was the slimy mud at the water's edge.

"You took your time," said a voice behind him. "We've been standing in this stinking mud for ages!"

Kipper looked round. Biff and Wilf were standing under some wooden steps that led down to a landing stage.

Biff sniffed the air. "Thanks, Tyler, for dropping us in it!" she joked. They all started to laugh. But as they did, a coldness touched them for a moment. Biff shivered.

Above them came the sound of voices.
Quickly, they hid in the shadow of the
steps. Three men came down, talking loudly.

"We can't be late," one of them said.
"Waterman!" he shouted at a passing boat.
At once it turned and headed towards them.

"Take us to the Globe," the first man
ordered as they all got in.

Suddenly, one of the men turned and stared into the shadows where the children were hiding. Had he seen them? If he had, it was too late. The boat was already heading out into the river.

Chapter 3

"Virans!" hissed Wilf. "I'm sure of it."
The moment they lost sight of the boat
on the busy river, Tyler's crackly voice came
from Biff's Link.

"You need to cross the river. But you can't
get a boat. You have no money. There's
only one bridge. It'll be packed with traffic –
carts, animals, people, stalls. It's a bit mad."

The children raced towards the bridge. The cobbled street was slippery and uneven. It was hard to run safely. "Tyler! The Virans talked about a 'Globe'?" Biff panted into her Link as they ran.

"It's a theatre," crackled Tyler's voice. "I'll send you a download."

Tyler was right. The bridge was busy, with smoky stalls, carts and horses, and packed ale houses. Everywhere they looked there were people. At one point they even had to push through a great crowd of people watching a huge black bear in chains being made to dance.

At last they reached the Globe Theatre.
A company of actors was standing in the
doorway talking to a man dressed in black.

They watched as the three Virans went up
to the man. One of them gave him a curt
bow.

Wilf's Link pinged. "Wow!" he gasped.
"Tyler says to look out for a man in black.
It might be Shakespeare! We need to get
closer. Come on!"

"I hear you need actors for your play, Mr
Shakespeare," said one of the Virans.

"So it *is* Shakespeare," said Wilf. "And he's
hiring actors. I have an idea."

Chapter 4

Shakespeare beamed at Kipper and Wilf. "Wonderful!" he said. "You're just what we need! You two can play the queen's ladies."

Shakespeare turned on his heel. "Hurry! We perform this afternoon."

They watched as the actors started to follow Shakespeare into the theatre.

"Nice one, Wilf," moaned Kipper. "The queen's ladies! Couldn't he see we're boys?"

The actor playing the queen turned to Kipper. "So? I'm a boy too!" He took off his wig. "My name is Jack. I always play the queen."

"That's silly," said Biff. "It would be better if a girl played it."

"Now, that *is* silly," laughed Jack. "A girl acting? Ridiculous!"

As they went inside the theatre, Wilf suddenly felt cold. He nodded towards the three Virans. "What parts are they going to play?" he asked Jack.

"I'm not sure. Guards, I think. They're new, like you," replied Jack.

Wilf looked at Kipper. "Then we need to be on guard too," he muttered.

Chapter 5

They watched the Virans closely all through the rehearsal.

"What are they up to?" muttered Kipper. "What can they do here? It's just a play."

Jack overheard what Kipper was saying.

"This is not just any play," he said. "We are doing this one for Queen Elizabeth. She loves the theatre. Sometimes she even comes in secret to watch us rehearse."

At that moment an old woman wearing a hooded cloak came into the theatre. She took the cloak off and handed it to Shakespeare. "All kneel for Queen Elizabeth!" he shouted.

"So that's it!" breathed Biff. "They're after the Queen."

The Queen came over to Jack. "I will be watching the play," she said. She gave Jack a knowing smile. "It will amuse me to see how you play the queen." She turned to the other actors. "Good luck to you all!" Everyone cheered.

From where she was sitting, Biff looked round at the Virans. They were whispering.

"The play will begin soon," called Shakespeare. "I want everyone ready."

But everyone was not ready. As the play was about to start, Jack went missing.

Chapter 6

Kipper was terrified. He was standing in Jack's costume and was about to go on stage.

Jack had not been found, so the start of the play had been delayed. Kipper had been told to replace him but he hadn't been able to learn the lines in time.

Luckily, Tyler had found a copy of the play in the library. He was going to whisper the queen's lines to Kipper through his Link.

The children could tell that the theatre was packed. There were shouts, cheers and boos as the play got underway.

Biff and Wilf peeked through the inner curtain. On the side of the stage, Queen Elizabeth was sitting watching the play. Two of the Virans had moved quite close to her.

"I don't like the look of it," said Wilf. "What's their game?"

"And where's Jack?" asked Kipper.

"Okay, Kipper. Get ready," said Tyler. "Your first line is, 'How fares our noble uncle?' Ready ... Go!"

Kipper took a deep breath. The inner curtain opened and he stepped on stage.

Before Kipper had time to open his mouth there was loud bang. A huge puff of smoke rose up from the front of the stage. A trap door opened underneath Queen Elizabeth's chair and she fell through it.

"They've made their move!" shouted Wilf. Through the smoke, he could see the two Virans about to jump through the trap door after the Queen.

"Zap them," yelled Biff. She threw her Zaptrap towards the escaping Virans. Wilf did the same.

The Zaptraps shot across the stage like tiny comets. They circled the two Virans with jagged blue flames. They transformed them into sparks of light.

"Got them!" shouted Biff.

The audience were amazed. They had never seen a play like this before.

"There's another Viran below the stage," yelled Kipper. He ran across to the trap door and dived through it. Biff and Wilf grabbed their Zaptraps and followed. Under the stage, they crashed to the floor. It was hard to see. The air was full of smoke and dust. A shaft of light cut through the gloom. There was a hole in the back wall.

"This way!" shouted Wilf. "He's blasted his way out."

They clambered out through the hole and onto the river bank. But it was too late.

The Viran had dragged Queen Elizabeth into a boat and was rowing out to the middle of the river. They were heading downstream, fast.

"I'll use my Zaptrap!" shouted Kipper, but it was in his pocket. He had been buttoned and sewn into his stage costume, and he couldn't get at it.

Chapter 7

The theatre had emptied. Everyone was on the river bank. No one knew what to do. Some soldiers had taken another boat onto the river. But they were a long way behind.

Kipper's Link crackled. It was Tyler. "If you hurry, you'll catch them at the bridge."

They dashed to the bridge. "I've got an idea!" Kipper shouted. He pulled the wire from his Link. He tied a hitch-knot to one of the bridge posts. It was a long way down. "What are you going to do?" asked Biff.

"Maybe I can swing down on the wire and grab the Queen just as the boat goes through," said Kipper.

But Kipper didn't need to. As the boat
shot under the bridge, the Queen grabbed
a chain trailing into the river. She hauled
herself up it easily, like an acrobat.

"That's weird," said Biff. "Surely she's not
strong enough to do that?"

The Queen flipped over the rail, gave
a bow and pulled off her wig. It was not
Queen Elizabeth. It was Jack.

At the same time, another queen appeared on the bridge. This was the real Queen – Queen Elizabeth I.

"Three queens?" said Biff, looking at Kipper.

A small, thin man stepped from behind Elizabeth. "More of a theatrical trick, really," he said. "I am Lord Cecil. My job is to foil plots against the Queen."

"The real Queen Elizabeth didn't go to the play," continued Lord Cecil. "We knew about a plot to kidnap her, so the young actor, Jack, took her place."

"Which meant Kipper had to take *my* place," smiled Jack.

"Thanks for nothing," snorted Kipper.

"But what about the kidnappers?" asked Jack.

Biff looked at the others. "Two of them have been dealt with, but one is still on the loose."

"He'll be well away by now," said Lord Cecil. "It was a fast tide!"

"He'll be back, though," said Biff quietly.

Queen Elizabeth turned to go. "Well, thank you one and all," she said. "I will send Lord Cecil to the theatre to reward you."

Wilf pressed his Link. "Portal position please, Tyler. The show's over. We're coming home."

Tyler's Mission Report

Location:	Date:
London	1601 AD
Mission Status:	Viran Status:
Viran plot foiled.	2 captured / 1 escaped.

Notes: Don't remind Kipper that he wore a dress. It really winds him up.

Kings and queens are like actors. They often wear posh costumes and perform ceremonies. The clothes make them look rich and powerful. Of course, it wasn't always good to be centre of attention. Often before a battle, soldiers were ordered to dress up as the king to confuse the enemy. I wouldn't fancy that job, I can tell you! Dressing up. Pretending to be someone else. That's theatre, right? ... Well, not always!

Sign off: ....Tyler.....................

History: downloaded !
Elizabethan Theatre

Shakespeare

Theatre in Elizabethan England was all about pretending. Nowhere else could boys dress up as girls, and the poorest of actors pretend to be a rich lord, a priest or even a king or queen.

The trouble was that sometimes the pretending was so good, many people thought the theatre could be dangerous. What if the crowds that packed into the theatres actually believed what they saw? What if the plays they watched made them angry or violent?

As a result, the government kept a tight control on the theatre. Women, for example, were not allowed to become actors. That is why boys had to play female roles.

Watching a play at the new Globe Theatre today

An old sketch of the Globe Theatre in London

Before they were staged, plays had to be read by a government official. He crossed out any words that might be critical of anything English, especially the Queen, the government and the church.

Despite this, some people still tried to use the theatre to spread anger amongst the crowds. For example, in 1601 Queen Elizabeth was nearly overthrown by a rebellion that began after the staging of a play called *King Richard the Second*.

For more information see the Time Chronicles website:
www.oxfordprimary.co.uk/timechronicles

Glossary

company *(page 17)* Here, a company means a group of actors who work together putting on a play. *A company of actors was standing in the doorway ...*

hiring *(page 18)* Employing. "... he's hiring actors."

'How fares our noble uncle?' *(page 27)* A line from *King Richard the Second*, a Shakespeare play. It means, *How are you, dear uncle?*

landing stage *(page 11)* A wooden platform built above the level of the river, used for getting on and off boats. *Biff and Wilf were standing under some wooden steps that led down to a landing stage.*

putrid *(page 10)* Rotten, foul smelling. *A putrid smell filled his nostrils.*

rehearse *(page 22)* To practise a play for a public performance. *Sometimes she even comes in secret to watch us rehearse.*

waterman *(page 12)* A waterman works on the river. Watermen used to take people along the river, a bit like taxi-drivers. *"Waterman!" he shouted at a passing boat.*

Thesaurus: Another word for ...
putrid *(page 10)* rancid, mouldy, rank, foul.

Have you read them all yet?

Level 11:

Level 12:

Time Runners

Tyler: His Story

A Jack and Three Queens

Mission Victory

The Enigma Plot

The Thief Who Stole Nothing

More great fiction from Oxford Children's:

www.winnie-the-witch.com

www.dinosaurcove.co.uk

About the Authors

Roderick Hunt MBE - creator of best-loved characters Biff, Chip, Kipper, Floppy and their friends. His first published stories were those he told his two sons at bedtime. Rod lives in Oxfordshire, in a house not unlike the house in the Magic Key adventures. In 2008, Roderick received an MBE for services to education, particularly literacy.

Roderick Hunt's son **David Hunt** was brought up on his father's stories and knows the world of Biff, Chip and Kipper intimately. His love of history and a good story has sparked many new ideas, resulting in the *Time Chronicles* series. David has had a successful career in the theatre, most recently working on scripts for Jude Law's *Hamlet* and *Henry V,* as well as Derek Jacobi's *Twelfth Night.*

Joint creator of the best-loved characters Biff, Chip, Kipper, Floppy and their friends, **Alex Brychta MBE** has brought each one to life with his fabulous illustrations, which are known and loved in many schools today. Following the Russian occupation of Czechoslovakia, Alex Brychta moved with his family from Prague to London. He studied graphic design and animation, before going to work on animation for Sesame Street. Since then he has devoted many years of his career to *Oxford Reading Tree,* bringing detail, magic and humour to every story! In 2012 Alex received an MBE for services to children's literature.

Roderick Hunt and Alex Brychta won the prestigious Outstanding Achievement Award at the Education Resources Awards in 2009.

43

Levelling info for parents

What do the levels mean?

Read with Biff Chip & Kipper First Chapter Books have been designed by educational experts to help children develop as readers.

Each book is carefully levelled to allow children to make gradual progress and to feel confident and enjoy reading.

The Oxford Levels you will see on these books are used by teachers and are based on years of research in schools. Below is a summary of what each Oxford Level means, so that you can help your child to improve and enjoy their reading.

The books at Level 11 (Brown Book Band):

At this level, the sentence structures are becoming longer and more complex. The story plot may be more involved and there is a wider vocabulary. However, the proportion of unknown words used per paragraph/page is still carefully controlled to help build their reading stamina and allow children to read independently.

This level mostly covers characterisation through characters' actions and words rather than through description. The story may be organised in various ways, e.g. chronologically, thematically, sequentially, as relevant to the text type and subject.

The books at Level 12 (Grey Book Band):

At this level, the sentences are becoming more varied in structure and length. Though still straightforward, more inference may be required, e.g. in dialogue to work out who is speaking. Again, the story may be organised in various ways: chronologically, thematically, sequentially, etc., so that children can reflect on how the organisation helps the reader to understand the text.

The *Times Chronicles* books are also ideal for older children who feel less confident and need more practice in order to build stamina. The text is written to be age and ability appropriate, but also engaging, motivating and funny, making them a pleasure for children to read at this stage of their reading development.

OXFORD
UNIVERSITY PRESS

Great Clarendon Street, Oxford, OX2 6DP,
United Kingdom

Oxford University Press is a department of the University of Oxford.
It furthers the University's objective of excellence in research, scholarship,
and education by publishing worldwide. Oxford is a registered trade mark
of Oxford University Press in the UK and in certain other countries

First published 2010
This edition published in 2015

British Library Cataloguing in Publication Data
Data available

978-0-19-273913-1

1 3 5 7 9 10 8 6 4 2

Paper used in the production of this book is a natural, recyclable product
made from wood grown in sustainable forests. The manufacturing process
conforms to the environmental regulations of the country of origin.

Printed in China

Acknowledgements: The publisher and authors would like to thank the following for
their permission to reproduce photographs and other copyright material:

P5tl Blaz Kure/Shutterstock; **P5tr** Ragnarock/Shutterstock; **P5ml** Mary Evans Picture
Library/Alamy; **P38** Ragnarock/Shutterstock; **P39** Valentin Agapov; **P39tl** TSR/Shutter-
stock; **P39tr** Leigh Prather/Shutterstock; **P39ml** Classic Image/Alamy; **P39bl** North Wind
Picture Archives/Alamy; **P40tr** Travelshots.com/Alamy; **P40bl** Classic Image/Alamy;
P39-40 Blaz Kure/Shutterstock; **P39-40** Jakub Krechowicz; **P39-40** Picsfive/Shutterstock;
P41 Blaz Kure/Shutterstock.

Book quiz answers

1 c
2 Queen Elizabeth I, Jack and Kipper.
3 By opening a trap door under her chair.